# Wynken, Blynken, & Nod

### A Poem by Eugene Field

### Illustrated by Johanna Westerman

TO JOHN

Published in the United States
by NorthSouth Books Inc., New York 10016.
Published simultaneously in Great Britain, Canada,
Australia, and New Zealand by NorthSouth Books Inc.,
an imprint of NordSüd Verlag AG,
CH-8050 Zürich, Switzerland.
First paperback edition published in 1998.

Library of Congress Cataloging-in-Publication Data
Field, Eugene, 1850-1895.
Wynken, Blynken and Nod: a poem / Eugene Field;
Illustrated by Johanna Westerman.
Summary: In this bedtime poem, three fishermen in
a wooden shoe catch stars in their nets of silver and gold.
1. Children's poetry, American. 2. Sleep—Juvenile poetry.
[1. American poetry.] I. Westerman, Johanna, ill. II. Title.
PS1667.W8 1995
811'.4—dc20 95-11692

A CIP record for this book is available from
The British Library

ISBN: 978-1-55858-422-8 (Trade binding)
13  15  17  19  21  TB  22  20  18  16  14
ISBN 978-1-55858-998-8 (paperback edition)
11  13  15  17  19  PB  20  18  16  14  12

The type is Marigold
The art was painted with watercolors
Typography by Marc Cheshire
Printed in Germany, September 2020.

Wynken, Blynken, and Nod one night
Sailed off in a wooden shoe—

Sailed on a river of crystal light,
Into a sea of dew.

"Where are you going, and what do you wish?"
The old moon asked the three.
"We have come to fish for the herring fish
That live in this beautiful sea;
Nets of silver and gold have we!"
Said Wynken,
Blynken,
And Nod.

The old moon laughed and sang a song,
As they rocked in the wooden shoe,

And the wind that sped them all night long
Ruffled the waves of dew.

The little stars were the herring fish
That lived in that beautiful sea—

"Now cast your nets wherever you wish—
Never afeard are we!"
So cried the stars to the fishermen three:
Wynken,
Blynken,
And Nod.

All night long their nets they threw
To the stars in the twinkling foam—

Then down from the skies came the wooden shoe,
Bringing the fishermen home;

'Twas all so pretty a sail it seemed
As if it could not be,
And some folks thought 'twas a dream they'd dreamed
Of sailing that beautiful sea—
But I shall name you the fishermen three:
Wynken,
Blynken,
And Nod.

Wynken and Blynken are two little eyes,
And Nod is a little head,
And the wooden shoe that sailed the skies
Is a wee one's trundle-bed.

So shut your eyes while mother sings
Of wonderful sights that be,
And you shall see the beautiful things
As you rock in the misty sea,

Where the old shoe rocked the fishermen three:
Wynken, Blynken, and Nod.